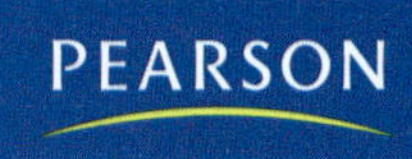

Jon Scieszka's TRUCKTOWN on Reading Street

A NAP

PEARSON

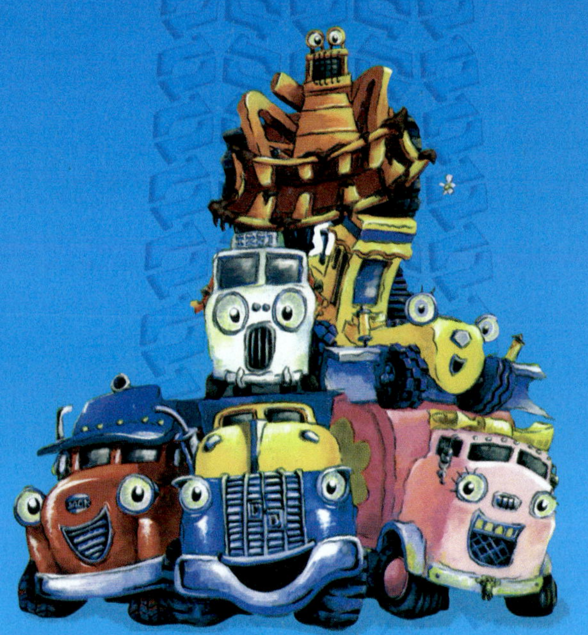

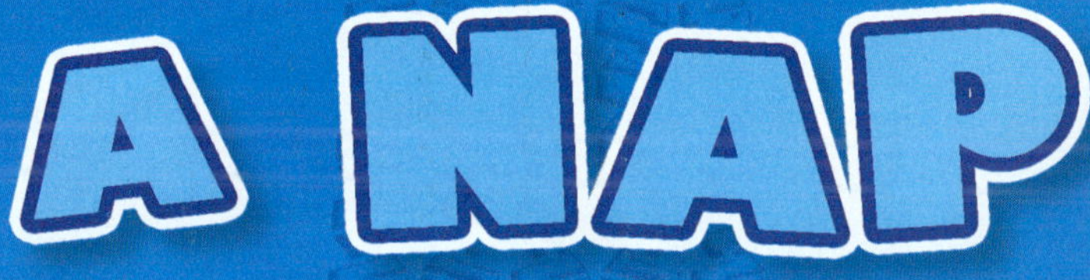

Glenview, Illinois • Boston, Massachusetts • Chandler, Arizona
Shoreview, Minnesota • Upper Saddle River, New Jersey

Rita was on a trip.

The sun had just set.

Where will Rita nap?

Rita can see a little hill.
"I will nap on it," she said.
And she did.

The sun was up a bit.

"I will still nap," said Rita.

But Rita did not!

Rita felt the hill tip!
Rita felt the hill zip!
Rita did not nap!

"I am not on a hill!" said Rita.

"I am on Big Rig!

Big, bad Big Rig!"

Jump fast Rita!

Rita did!

Did Big Rig see Rita?
Big Rig did not.
Rita was glad!